# Something Else to Want

To Lori,
Blessings & enjoy!
Darliss Batchelor

# Something Else to Want

Darliss Batchelor

Word in Due Season
Publishing, LLC

# Something Else to Want

Darliss Batchelor



Word in Due Season Publishing, LLC
P.O. Box 210921
Auburn Hills, Michigan 48321-0921
www.DarlissBatchelor.com
wids-pub@comcast.net

Cover Design by AMB Branding and Design
ambbranding@gmail.com

ISBN 13: 978-0-9829686-2-8

Library of Congress Control Number: 2016902695

Printed in the United States of America

To all those who refuse to be bound by tradition.

Be you.

# *Acknowledgements*

God, the Father, who entrusted this gift and responsibility of writing. I'm learning this assignment is not about me, but about the souls attached to each project. Thank You for your trust.

My husband for his endless support. Without his understanding, this writing ministry would be difficult. I appreciate his willingness to make things easier.

My son and grandson for providing additional motivation for me to continue. I know they're always watching.

I realize that I have been remiss in previous acknowledgements by not mentioning the ministries that have played a major role in my life. Anointed Word Ministries led by Gregory & Patricia Heathman and Redeemed Christian Church led by Kenneth Sr. and Sylvia Anthony.

I've come to understand that the editing process improves both the writing and the writer. I appreciate the editors for this project, SJS Editorial Design and Critique Editing Services. I appreciate each of them for their contributions to this project.

I would also like to send a big "God bless you" to my family and friends who support my writing ministry. Many of you not only read my work and provide feedback, but you also share my work with others. I appreciate you all. I don't take any of you for granted.

# Something Else to Want

# *Dreaming*

Neely sat on the front porch of her family's north side Flint, Michigan duplex. Neely, her sister Evelyn, and their parents had lived there for as long as she could remember. The duplex faced a park, providing for a peaceful view. The thick wooden columns holding up the porch's ceiling were bright white, in contrast with the soft yellow on the rest of the house, courtesy of a recent painting afforded by her father's third shift factory job. She loved sitting there enjoying the breeze. She looked out over the front yard, past the road, and across the park into the horizon, letting her mind wander to its favorite place, her future. Her mind was there this afternoon when the scent of fried chicken drew her to the kitchen.

Neely made her way into the house and stood at the arched opening leading from the dining room to the kitchen, admiring the look of joy on her mother's face. She watched as her mother, Janis, dropped seasoned and floured chicken pieces into hot oil, stirred turnip greens, cut corn from the cob to be fried, and checked the cornbread seemingly all at the same time. Though sweat ran down her face and her body appeared fatigued, it was obvious she was satisfied. Content. This was her dream, not Neely's. Neely had other plans for her own heaven on Earth. Plans that disappointed her family, especially her father.

Janis looked up at Neely and smiled, placing her dimples on display. Neely and Janis were each other's mirror image. They had the same medium height, smooth dark chocolate skin, dimples, and expressive eyes. Their one difference? Their hair. Neely's thick black hair was styled in an afro, while her mother's was pressed and styled into tight pin curls. The hair at Janis' temples was a mixture of gray and red, courtesy of Miss Clairol. She wiped the mist from her forehead with the towel she had over the shoulder of her housedress.

"Don't just stand there. Make some Kool-Aid or something."

Neely decided not to fight her mother's request. She chose the packet containing red powder, dumped it into the glass pitcher along with sugar, and placed it under the faucet, filling it with cold water.

"Mama, can I ask you something?"

"Yes. Hand me that plate with the chicken on it."

Neely lifted the plate with several golden-fried pieces of chicken sitting on a paper towel. As her mother pulled more pieces out of the hot oil and laid them alongside the rest, Neely asked a question that had been burning in her heart.

"I know I'm not like Evelyn, but do you all hate me?"

Janis froze in place as she rubbed her hands up and down the front of her housedress.

"Watch that chicken. I'll be right back." Janis took a few steps to leave the room with Neely's question lingering in the air.

"Wait!" Neely yelled.

Her mother stopped, her back still facing her daughter.

"You never answered my question. Do you hate me?"

Janis turned toward her daughter with a concerned look on her face. "You know better than that," she said and left the room.

"Do I?" Neely asked herself, the only person left in the kitchen.

## *Not the Right Daughter for That*

Later in the evening, Neely read "The Feminine Mystique" in the bedroom she and her sister, Evelyn shared. The white walls displayed various posters of the Jackson 5 and The Temptations. The twin beds were covered with matching pink bedspreads and starched white sheets. She turned the page, revealing the end of the chapter she was reading when she overheard her name mentioned in her parents' room across the hall.

"Do you know where Neely is? I need her to iron this shirt for me real quick," Milton asked his wife.

"I don't know why you're looking for Neely. She is not the right daughter for that," Janis responded.

"She's 19 years old and needs to learn, Janis. Now, where is she?"

Neely rolled her eyes as she heard her parents discussing her. She hoped she would be able to finish the chapter before facing the continuing effort to 'make Neely into someone she's not.'

"She has no interest, Milton. Let it go. Give me the shirt and I'll iron it," Janis said.

"I done told you Neely is going to do it," Milton responded.

"Okay, you're just going to frustrate yourself. I think she's in her room."

Neely heard her father's footsteps as he headed across the hall, looking for her.

"What are you doing?" Milton asked.

"What do you need?" Neely looked up, closing her book.

"I need you to iron my shirt for me so I can get to work on time," he said, holding the shirt out to her.

"You know I don't do no ironing, Daddy. Get Evelyn to do that." Neely reopened her book.

"What you say? You betta get up and do what I told you to do. As long as you live under my roof, you don't get to decide what you don't do. Put that book down and take care of this shirt. That's why your mind all messed up now, reading all that kind of stuff."

Neely did as she was told and stomped past her father, grabbing his shirt.

"Hey," Milton said as he grabbed Neely by the arm. "Don't you ever tell me what you don't do around here. And you betta not roll your eyes at me either. I brought you into this world and I'll take you out. Don't think I won't just because you're a girl."

"Yes, Daddy."

"No man is going to want you if you can't be respectful. You need to take notes from Evelyn. I bet she'll be married before you if you don't get yourself together."

Neely went to the bathroom to get a towel to cover the heavy wooden dining room table while she ironed the shirt. She then went to get the iron. She laid the towel out and plugged the iron in. *It's so unfair how my parents treat me compared to my baby sister. Evelyn loves doing domestic stuff like ironing. Why should I be forced to do it?*

After waiting for the iron to heat, Neely positioned the shirt on the towel-covered table, picked up the iron, and moved it over the garment. She remembered seeing Evelyn use starch on her father's work shirts, so she left the room to retrieve it. When she returned, she found Evelyn lifting the iron from the shirt.

"What are you doing?" Neely asked her baby sister.

"Trying to keep you out of trouble."

"What are you talking about?"

"You walked away and left the iron on the shirt. You can't do that," Evelyn said as she lifted the shirt from the table.

"I forgot to get the starch. What's the big deal?"

"Don't you know you can burn the shirt leaving a hot iron on it like that?" Evelyn asked, showing Neely the light brown mark left on the bleached-white shirt. "When Daddy finds out, he's going to be mad."

"I told him I didn't want to do this in the first place. But no, everyone's intent on me learning how to be a good wife."

"Neely," Evelyn whispered. "You need to come down off that high horse. You're a woman and if you're lucky, a man will want to make you his wife. What you want to do is not realistic. It's not going to happen, Neely, and the sooner you accept that, the better off you'll be."

"Is my shirt done?" Milton asked as he rushed through the living room toward the dining room.

"Um, yeah. I mean, no," Neely stuttered.

Milton picked up the half-ironed, slightly scorched shirt,

noticing the tinge left behind by the hot iron.

"I know this shirt ain't burned!" Milton yelled.

"It was my fault. I accidentally burned the shirt," Evelyn explained. "I saw Neely struggling with it and, well, I was just trying to help."

Milton glared at Neely and said, "I don't care who burned the shirt. I told *you* to iron it. Get on upstairs, girl, and I'll be up there to deal with you in a minute. You gonna make me late for work."

Neely turned to do as she was told and to wait for her punishment. She looked back over her shoulder at her father and sister as she approached the stairs.

Milton placed an arm around Evelyn's shoulder. "This ain't your fault, Evelyn. I know you were just trying to take up for your big sister. You're a good girl. I wish Neely was more like you. She's gonna be living in my house forever. Ain't no man gonna want a prideful and high-minded woman like her."

Neely ran up the stairs with tears in her eyes. *Why can't my family just accept me? Why does everything come down to getting a husband? I'm not sure if I ever want a husband, but certainly not yet. Why do I need a man? I have a plan and I'm smart enough to make it happen. I want to postpone marriage and family to go to college, get a degree in management, and earn my own money. If I need something fixed, I'll hire someone. Other than that, what does a man really bring to the table? No matter what happens, I am determined to prove everyone wrong. No longer are women only suited to be barefoot and pregnant housewives. It's 1970, a new day and a new time with more opportunities for women. Women don't have to count on a man to succeed in life and I'm going to prove that point.*

## *You Don’t Think I Care?*

Neely descended the stairs and walked through the living room and dining room into the kitchen. After seeing Evelyn there, she grabbed an apple from the bowl of fruit on the counter and turned to head back upstairs.

“Hey. You’re going to act like I’m not standing here?” Evelyn asked, waving her arms in Neely’s face.

“That was the plan,” Neely responded.

“I hope Daddy wasn’t too hard on you yesterday.”

“No harder than usual. Why do you care?” Neely asked as she leaned against the kitchen counter.

“You don’t think I care? Is that why you’re so mean to me?”

“I was never mean to you.” Neely frowned.

“You put mouthwash in my toy teacup, told me it was mint tea, and I ended up drunk.”

"I guess that was a little mean," Neely admitted, sharing a laugh with Evelyn.

"We won't talk about you giving my bike away, breaking my doll's head off, and other stuff you did." Evelyn took Neely's hand in hers. "All I ever wanted was for us to be like sisters."

"You don't know what it's like to be me in this family."

"I know Mama and Daddy give you a hard time, but they just want to make sure you're going to be okay."

"I'm going to college no matter what Mama and Daddy think. Then I'll be able to do whatever I need to do to take care of myself."

"I sure hope so, Neely," she said.

## *A Man That Could Make Me Change My Mind*

Neely entered Hamady Brothers, the neighborhood grocery store, to purchase some things her mother needed. First she went to the canned goods aisle to purchase a few cans of Spam, her father's favorite. She looked at her list and decided to pick up bread next. She looked up and found a young man standing there, smiling at her. He was a little taller than she was and had a smile that caused her heart to leap.

"Excuse me," Neely said to the smiling man, running her hand through her blown-out afro.

"Um, I was just standing here admiring you while you were picking up your groceries."

"Thank you." Neely smiled.

"You're welcome."

Silence ensued as the two stood awkwardly in the canned food aisle.

"I'm Julius. What's your name?"

"Neely." The rest of her words refused to leave her throat.

"That's a pretty name."

"I got it from my grandmother on my father's side."

Silence.

"You live around here?"

"Yes, right down the street." Neely pointed in the direction of her house.

"Do you mind if I walk you home?"

"I would like that. I have a few more things to pick up first, though."

"I'll wait for you outside."

"Okay." Neely smiled once again.

Neely and Julius lost track of time as the ten-minute walk became a thirty-minute adventure. The conversation was stimulating and exciting. Neely had never experienced interaction with a young man like this.

"Well, this is my house," Neely stated as they arrived at her family's home.

"Can we sit on the steps and talk for a few minutes?"

"Sure, let me take this stuff inside to my mother." Julius

handed Neely the groceries he had carried from the store.

Julius and Neely sat on the steps talking for the next hour. When her mother called her in for dinner, Julius stood to leave.

"Can I have your phone number so I can call you?"

"Okay." Neely recited her phone number.

"All right, I'll call you tonight."

"Not too late. My father won't let me use the phone after eight."

"I'll talk to you soon." He pulled her hand to his lips and planted a light kiss on it, all while keeping his eyes locked on hers.

Neely turned and walked up the steps to the house. Her thoughts turned to the romantic moment she just experienced. *Now this man could make me change my mind about getting married. I think I would marry him right now.*

## *It's for the Best*

Milton yelled from the living room couch after hearing a knock at the door, "Who is it?"

The knocking continued, causing him to rise and go to the door. Neely followed to find Julius standing there. His skin was the color of toasted pecans, his eyes wide and his thick lips brought a smile to her face. She was so excited he actually came by to visit her like he said he would.

"What can I do for you?" Milton asked, appraising the young man.

"I'm Julius, Mr. Evans and I'd like to see Neely, sir."

Neely watched as recognition came over her father's face.

"You're John's boy, ain't you?"

"Yes, sir, I am. You know my people?" Julius asked, placing a foot up on a step and leaning one arm on the railing.

"I know 'em good. Your daddy and me used to work together. Tell him I said hi."

"I will."

"Say, uh son, you said you're here for Neely?"

"Yes, sir."

"Look here, son. If you're looking for a wife, you picked the wrong daughter. Don't nobody want Neely. Evelyn's the one you want. Let me get her."

"But I like Neely."

"You won't once you talk to Evelyn. She'll make a good wife and mother. She's a good girl."

Milton turned around and came face-to-face with Neely's tear-stained face. Dropping his head, he whispered to Neely as he approached her, "Neely, go get your sister. It's for the best."

# *I Want That Man*

Neely walked up the stairs leading to the front door of the family's home. She entered the living room and found Julius there, sitting on the floral couch.

"Hello," he said, rising from his seat.

"Hi," she responded. "Um, what are you doing here?"

"I'm here visiting your sister," he said, returning to his seat.

"Oh." Neely turned to leave the room.

"Neely, wait a minute." Neely stopped. Julius approached her. "I'm sorry about what happened."

"Sure you are," Neely said, turning to stand before Julius with folded arms.

"No, I really am. You saw what your father did."

"Yeah, but he didn't *make* you date my sister."

"Okay, you're right."

"I know I'm right. How does she feel about our relationship?"

"Umm...," he said, rubbing a hand across the back of his neck.

"You didn't tell her?"

"What is there to tell? You and I talked a few times but that's it."

Neely swallowed hard as she realized she was so easily replaced. She bit her bottom lip and blinked her eyes to destroy the evidence of her hurt feelings. *Here I was thinking Julius was the one man worth putting my plans on hold. Yet. as soon as he met Evelyn, he forgot all about me.*

"Hey, Neely," Evelyn said as she came into the room. "What did you just say about you and Julius?"

Julius' hands stuffed his pockets and his eyes shot to the burgundy-sculpted shag carpet.

"What?" Evelyn asked again, then folded her arms and looked from Neely to Julius.

"Can I talk to you in the kitchen for a minute?" Neely asked.

"Sure. Excuse me, Julius. I'll be right back."

"He's so cute, isn't he?" Evelyn squealed upon arriving in the kitchen.

"Yeah, yeah, yeah. I need to tell you something."

"Neely, he's got a brother," Evelyn whispered. "Maybe we can double date sometime." Evelyn paused a moment and looked into her sister's eyes. "I'm sorry I got so excited. What did you need to tell me?"

Neely took a few steps before saying, "I met Julius weeks ago. He came to see me one day and Daddy basically took him from me and gave him to you."

"Daddy would never do that." After a brief pause, Evelyn chuckled. "I can't believe this."

"What?"

"You're jealous."

"Why would I be jealous?"

"Because deep down inside, you really do want a man. You're allowed to change your mind."

"I didn't change my mind. I thought you needed to know the truth."

"Don't worry, Neely. I got you covered. I'll introduce you to Julius' brother," Evelyn said as she patted her big sister on her arm.

"I don't want Julius' brother." *I want Julius.*

Evelyn left the room to return to her guest as Neely followed, heading to the bedroom.

*Dating Julius' brother might be a good idea since my parents seem dead-set on me being somebody's wife, too. It just might distract them while I work on getting into college.*

## *Something Else to Want*

Neely went into the closet she and Evelyn shared in search of something to wear for their double date with Julius and his brother, Gerald. Janis, hearing the noise, came into the room to see what was going on.

"What are you doing?" Her mother asked, peeking through the door.

"I'm looking for something to wear on a date tonight," Neely responded, holding a dashiki over a denim skirt, laying the ensemble across the bed.

"Why do you have to be so militant all of the time? Why don't you wear a nice dress? I'll even press your hair."

"This is who I am. He'll have to take me or leave me.

"So who are you going out with?"

"Julius' brother, Gerald. Julius and Evelyn are going too."

"Well your father will love hearing this."

"Good, maybe he'll get off my back," Neely blurted out.

"Neely, I'm going to ask you something personal. Do you like boys or are you funny?" Janis asked candidly as she perched herself on one of the twin beds in the room.

"No, I'm not funny. I'm just focused and I don't want a man getting in the way," Neely responded as she joined her mother on the bed.

"Why do you think a man will keep you from doing what you want?"

"When you were growing up, was it your dream to get married and have kids?" Neely asked her mother. Janis responded by wiping her hands on her housedress.

"Mama, was it?"

"Wasn't nothing else to want then, child!" Janis yelled, slamming her hands onto the front of her thighs.

"Why not?" Neely questioned.

"We were raised to take care of a house and family. It's what women are supposed to do, not try to be the boss over men like you want to do."

"Who told you that?"

"My daddy, just like your daddy is trying to tell you."

"See, that's why I say a man would stand in my way. They all got the same idea of what a woman is *supposed* to do. I know you're doing what you were taught; but, I also know you're not fulfilled. I don't want to end up that way," Neely said as she got up and looked through the closet for shoes to match her ensemble.

"Neely, baby, you act like being a housewife is a bad thing. Don't you want a nice strong young man to take care of you and to love you?"

"There's something else to want now, Mama. Something else to want," Neely said.

## *Let the Games Begin*

"Man, I appreciate you and Evelyn setting this date up for me," Gerald said as he waited next to his brother in the living room of the Evans' home.

"You're welcome," Julius responded.

"If she looks anything like Evelyn, this could turn out great. I enjoyed the conversation," Gerald said.

"Neely is darker than Evelyn and looks more like their mother."

Gerald swiveled his torso to look fully at Julius. "What does that mean? Is she ugly?"

"No, she's pretty."

"Pretty? Man, that's just another word for ugly. There's only one thing pretty and dark can do for me," Gerald stated.

"Man, that's my girlfriend's sister," Julius responded.

Neely and Evelyn stood shoulder to shoulder at the top of the steps listening to the conversation.

Evelyn elbowed her sister. "Don't pay that no mind. He's going to like you. Watch," Evelyn said.

Neely went down the stairs with Evelyn following. When her eyes met Gerald's, his eyes lit up as if the heavens had opened up and the angels sang. Neely chuckled as she stepped in front of ain't-but-one-thing-pretty-and-dark-can-do-for-me Gerald.

"All right, let's go," Julius said, grabbing Evelyn's hand as Gerald remained in a trance, mouth open and eyes bulging. Julius returned, patted him on his arm, and said, "Come on."

***

The quartet settled in at their table at Walli's Supper Club. The hostess provided them with menus and walked away. After perusing the various food items available, Neely turned her attention to Gerald. He wasn't nearly as handsome as Julius. His skin was the color of maple syrup. His round face held a clown-like smile that perturbed Neely for some reason.

"Do you need something, my love?" Gerald asked Neely.

"Uh, no," Neely said as she broke her stare and looked back at the menu.

The waitress arrived at the table to take their orders. She looked around the table to determine who would go first. Her eyes finally landed on Evelyn.

"Ma'am, are you ready to order?"

Closing her menu and handing it to the waitress, she responded, "Yes, I would like a hamburger and fries."

"Ma'am, what would you like?" the waitress asked Neely.

"I would like the steak," Neely said.

"Neely, do you know how much that costs?" Evelyn whispered. "You need to order something else."

"No, I want a steak. Is that okay with you, Gerald?" Neely asked, smiling at her date.

Gerald pulled his wallet from his pocket and looked through the money in it. "I don't think I can afford to feed you and me too if you get a steak."

Neely leaned toward her date. "But, I really want that steak," she said as her lashes fluttered.

Gerald leaned toward Neely. "You can have whatever you want. I'll eat at home later." He puckered his lips and closed his eyes.

"How would you like your steak cooked?" Neely returned her attention to the waitress, ignoring Gerald's advance.

"I would like it medium. Thank you. Don't forget the baked potato with extra butter and sour cream, please." She closed her menu and handed it to the waitress.

Gerald released the pucker in his lips and opened his eyes. Neely noticed his disappointment, but felt no remorse. He had been willing to discard her just like all the other guys. His reasons may have been different, but Neely's sense of rejection wasn't.

"Get what you want, Gerald. I'll pay for your meal," Julius said, shaking his head.

Evelyn grabbed Neely's hand, pulled her up from the table, and asked to be excused from the table. She dragged her across the dining room, heading to the hideaway for women. Once they were inside the ladies room, she turned to face her big sister.

"I am so embarrassed," she said with her hands firmly placed on her hips. "I can't believe you would order a meal that expensive knowing he won't be able to eat because of it. You know he doesn't have that kind of money."

"He thought I would be ugly because of my dark skin," Neely responded with her own venom. "You wouldn't understand how that feels."

"Oh, so you're teaching him a lesson, huh?"

"Yes, and it's one he's going to learn over and over again, every time we go out."

"That is so mean, Neely. You know he likes you."

"I know."

Evelyn shook her head and spoke to Neely, "It's not your dark skin that makes you ugly. As beautiful as you are on the outside, no one would ever know the ugliness you have on the inside of you." Evelyn sneered as she backed toward the exit.

"You haven't seen ugly yet, little sister," Neely said, matching Evelyn's anger as she whisked past her and exited the ladies room.

## *So, How About That Movie?*

The phone rang for the fiftieth time in 30 minutes. Neely knew because she counted each ring while sitting in the living room watching TV. Heavy footsteps overhead stopped at the top of the stairs.

"Don't make me come down there, Neely. You betta answer that phone. You know I got to go to work tonight," Milton grumbled.

"It's just Gerald. He won't stop bugging me."

Milton came partway down the stairs and leaned over the stair rail. "You ought to be glad he's interested. That boy came by here looking for you and your mama said you wouldn't even come downstairs to see what he wanted." The phone stopped ringing.

"He keeps telling me I'm his wife, but I don't want to get married."

"Something is really wrong with you."

"I have a plan."

"You got a plan to live in my house for the rest of your life. That's your plan. Got a good young man who wants to marry you and you talkin' about your plan."

"This is why I don't want a man," Neely said as the phone began ringing again. "He's too needy and he's got too much time on his hands. I don't have time to talk on the phone and be with him like he wants. This is just too much."

"He'd make a good husband. If it's him, talk to that boy. I'm trying to get some sleep," Milton demanded as we went upstairs.

"Hello?" Neely said as she answered the phone.

"Hi, honey. It's Gerald."

"Hi."

"I've been trying to reach you."

"You're going to have to stop calling like that. My father works nights so he's sleep around this time."

"I'm sorry. I won't do that again."

"Thank you. Now what did you want to talk to me about?"

"I wanted to know if you want to go to a movie with me Friday night."

"Gerald, I don't think we should date anymore."

"Why?" Gerald moaned.

"For one, you want to get married and I don't."

"We don't have to get married right now. I'm willing to wait as long as it takes. I'll never give up on us."

"Why are you making this so difficult?" Neely asked.

"Because you're worth it. We're worth it," Gerald stated. "So how about that movie?"

## *Dreams Do Come True*

"Neely, come on down here! You need to see this!" Janis yelled.

Neely reached the bottom of the stairs and saw Julius on one knee and Evelyn in tears. Evelyn's dream was about to come true; she was getting ready to be a wife.

*How could he ask Evelyn to marry him just four months after we met?*

"Evelyn, will you be my wife?" Julius asked.

Evelyn hesitated, looking around at her parents, but allowing her eyes to rest on her big sister the longest.

"Answer the man! Don't keep him waiting now, Evelyn," her father said.

"Only if Neely will stand up with me. What do you say?" Evelyn asked, returning her gaze to her sister.

"I done already told him he got my blessing. That's all you need. Neely ain't got nothing to say about this. Don't let her mess you up!" Milton said.

"Neely?" Evelyn asked once again.

Neely felt the eyes of everyone in the room on her, forcing her to answer on the spot.

"I'll do whatever you want me to do," Neely responded.

Evelyn's eyes misted once again as she returned her attention to Julius who shifted on his knee.

"Julius, I'll be your wife. I'll marry you."

Janis and Milton yelled their approval and hugged as though they were the newly engaged couple. Evelyn and Julius embraced a few seconds before Milton pushed them apart.

"Boy, you getting a little too close, aren't you? You ain't married to my daughter yet."

"When do y'all want to get married?" Milton asked.

"As soon as Evelyn is ready, sir," Julius responded.

"You're ready right now, ain't that right, Evelyn? I know she's only 17, but I'll sign," Milton said.

"No, we're going to plan a nice simple wedding for our baby girl. I think we can do that in about three months. Evelyn won't need our permission then," Janis said, gazing at her younger daughter with tears flowing down her face.

Neely slipped out of the room as the celebration began. She didn't feel the joy everyone else did. Julius and Evelyn were getting married. Milton and Janis would see one of their daughters living the "family dream." Neely was left second-guessing her decision to put marriage and family off for a bit. If she hadn't, maybe *she* would be marrying Julius instead of Evelyn.

## *Ain't No Shame in That*

"Neely, can you come over to our bedroom? We want to talk to you," Janis yelled from her bedroom door.

"I'm here," Neely stated as she rounded the corner into her parents' bedroom. "You want to talk to me?"

"Sit down for a minute."

Neely complied, sitting on the bed with her parents.

"I'll just get right to the point. Evelyn told us you've been ignoring her ever since she got engaged to Julius," Janis said.

"She said that?"

"Yes, she did. Do you want to tell us what's going on?"

"I don't want to talk about it," Neely said, lowering her head.

"Are you mad that she's getting married and you're not?" Janis asked.

"No. Well, maybe. I'm not sure."

"See, Janis? This girl is just as confused as she can be. She don't know what she wants. I'm about to clear it up for her," Milton stated.

"Calm down, Milton. This isn't helping."

"What? You think going to that college is gonna make you smarter than us? Listen here, you are going to be a housewife and a good one if I have anything to do with it," Milton said, losing his patience. "I'm not going to have people looking at me all cross-eyed thinking I raised a high-minded daughter. No, I'm not going to have it. You're going to do what I tell you."

"I thought we agreed to listen and be patient," Janis reminded Milton.

"I can't, Janis. It brings shame to my name for this girl to be an old maid living in this house. I am ashamed of you," Milton said, pointing at Neely.

"Milton!" Janis shouted.

"No, Janis. I mean it. I don't know where *you* went wrong, raising a daughter like her. She should be more like Evelyn. She acts like she's too good to be a wife and mother. Ain't no shame in that. None that I can think of."

"Honey, don't pay attention to your father. He's just a little upset. We love you and we want to see you live a good life. We just don't want to see you get hurt," Janis said, reaching for her daughter's hand.

"What could hurt more than my own father deciding I'm not good enough for Julius and giving him to Evelyn? I actually liked him."

"Milton! You did that?" Janis asked her husband.

"How was I supposed to know she liked him?" Milton shared as he dropped his head. "I did it because I didn't want her wasting that man's time," Milton stated, folding his arms.

"I liked Julius a lot and now he's marrying Evelyn all because of you."

"You don't want to be a wife no way."

"I don't know what may have happened with Julius, but now I'll never know."

"I'll tell you what would've happened. That man would've left you because you don't know how to take care of a family. That's what would've happened."

"I am so tired of you trying to force me to be something I'm not. I'm going to do what I set out to do. Once I leave this house, I'm never coming back again." Neely left the room, wiping tears from her eyes.

"Where you going? You're not ever leaving this house. If you do, you'll be back quicker than James Brown's feet," Milton yelled out to her.

Neely returned to the room, tears flooding her cheeks. "I wouldn't come back here for nothing in the world."

"We love you, baby," Janis said.

"You don't love me and I don't love you either." Neely turned once again to leave the room.

Milton launched off the bed, unbuckling the thick black belt around his waist. "You what? Now I know you done lost your mind. I'm going to give you something to hate me for." Milton released the belt from its loops and lunged in Neely's direction.

"Let her be, Milton," Janis said, restraining her husband.

"No, Janis. Ain't no way I can let that go. I shoulda done this a long time ago," Milton argued.

"We went about this all wrong. Just let things cool off a little."

"I think it's all wrong to let her talk to us like that. I should be in there right now fixin' that problem."

"We tried everything we know and it didn't change a thing. She's more determined now. I'm thinking we're gonna just have to stop fighting her on this," Janis resolved.

Neely returned to the room one final time. "One more thing, I'm ashamed of both of you and you should be ashamed of yourselves, too.

"What?" Janis responded.

"You should be ashamed for not wanting your child to do better than you." Neely watched as Janis' hand flew to her chest and Milton fumbled with his belt again before she left the room.

***

Neely ran into the hallway and bumped into Evelyn, almost knocking her down. The look of shock on Evelyn's face told Neely that Evelyn heard everything she and her parents said. She now knew Neely wasn't jealous, but had been telling the truth about her and Julius. Neely continued into the bedroom and fell across her bed, burying her face into her pillow.

## *You Like Him, but I Love Him*

Neely traveled through the living room, dining room, and kitchen, searching for her sister. The time had come for them to hash out the "Julius issue.” Neely hoped to alleviate the awkwardness that existed between her and her sister over the past two weeks. Neely looked out the kitchen door onto the back porch. Evelyn sat on the steps, looking like the love struck woman she was.

Neely went outside and sat next to her sister. Several moments passed before either said a word.

“Daddy was wrong for interfering with you and Julius’ relationship,” Evelyn said, breaking the silence.

“I agree. But I think Daddy got involved because he was looking out for you. He knew you couldn’t get a man without his help,” Neely sniped.

"That's what you think? I thought maybe it was God's way of bringing me and Julius together since you don't want to get married anyway," Evelyn calmly spoke.

"I could see myself marrying Julius, though. He's so smooth and considerate and he can have a conversation about anything. I liked him so much I was considering forgetting my plan, getting married and having his babies," Neely responded with a chuckle.

"You like him, but I love him." Evelyn looked at her sister. "He told me you two were just friends."

"We didn't get the chance to become more."

"I decided I'm going to marry him."

"How could you marry him knowing you weren't his first choice?"

"But he chose me, Neely. Now are you going to be upset?" Evelyn asked, ignoring Neely's question.

"You've made your decision so what does it matter how I feel?"

"Because I want to know."

"I don't know how I feel."

"Will you still stand up with me?"

"Maybe I will. Maybe I won't. We'll just have to see what happens." Neely left her sister sitting on the back porch as she re-entered the house.

*I hope Evelyn will give me some time to figure out my feelings before she presses me about dresses and everything. I need to decide whether I'm going to stand up for her or not.*

## *Tissue Paper Flowers and Cream Cheese Sandwiches*

Neely, Evelyn, and Janis stood over the boxes on the dining room table filled with tissue paper flowers made to put on the wedding cars. Three months had passed sooner than expected and the family was pressed to get everything done overnight.

"Well, tomorrow's the big day," Neely said as she twisted the tissue until it took the shape of a flower. She separated the layers, giving her creation more fullness.

"I can't wait to ride around tomorrow blowing our horns so people know our daughter got married," Janis said, smiling as she shared in the activity with her daughters.

"Isn't this enough?" Neely asked.  She sighed and placed the flower she'd just completed in one of five boxes full of them. She flexed her fingers to remove the stiffness.

"I want to make sure we have plenty. We'll use this last box of tissue and we'll be done with the flowers. Then we'll get started on the sandwiches for the reception," Janis said.

"Sandwiches?" Neely asked.

"Yes, we're making sandwiches out of colored cream cheese," Evelyn responded. "We'll spread different colored cream cheese between a few slices of bread, cut off the crusts, and cut the sandwiches into quarters. Then you'll get to see the colored layers inside."

"That's different," Neely said.

"I need to ask you something," Evelyn said.

"Okay," Neely responded.

"Are you going to be my maid of honor?" Evelyn asked, looking into her sister's eyes.

*How do I tell her I really don't even want to go to this wedding, never mind be a part of it?*

"Yes, I'll be there," Neely announced.

"Now everything will be perfect and I know Gerald will think so, too," Evelyn said.

## *It Could've Been Me*

Neely stood, looking toward the back of the church as Evelyn made her way toward the altar accompanied by their father. Milton was obviously honored to escort his daughter into the ideal future in his mind, marriage and then starting a family. Neely concentrated on maintaining her pasted-on smile as she observed her mother and twisted a lock of her hair so tightly it hurt. She sensed her pride that her youngest daughter was getting married. She then pointed her gaze toward her soon-to-be brother-in-law, Julius. She could see the joy he felt knowing he would soon marry the woman he loved.

Neely allowed her eyes to scan the rest of the room as Evelyn continued her trek. She couldn't remember seeing so many flowers in one place in her life. She knew they cost a whole lot more money than the family could afford. Neely couldn't understand their happiness. She wasn't impressed by this expression of love on display today. Neely felt it was much ado about nothing. Where was the joy in a family sacrificing as they had so Evelyn could get a big poufy dress, decorate this church, and feed all of these people colored cream cheese sandwiches? How could her parents be so excited when her father had had to work overtime almost around the clock at the truck plant to pay for this wedding? And why didn't anyone notice the anger *she* felt? After all, this could've been her wedding if her father hadn't interfered.

Evelyn finally reached the altar. Neely had to admit she made a stunning bride. Julius was handsome in his tux but seemed anxious, having to wait the few extra moments it took for Milton to give Evelyn's hand to him. The two looked at each other as though no one else was in the room. Neely still questioned Julius' decision. Based on their conversations, she knew Julius had a good head on his shoulders and seemed to know what he wanted in life; so, what did he want with Evelyn? Evelyn had no spunk, no backbone. She was boring, for goodness' sake, with all of that cooking and cleaning stuff. Why did Julius choose her when Neely was headed to college, intelligent, independent, interesting, exuberant, and had more going for her than knowing how to bake a perfect pie? What was so attractive about that? Neely finally concluded Julius wanted someone who would submit and meet his every need, someone who had no ambition and wanted no other identity beyond being his wife. Neely would never fall into that trap. Not ever. She concluded Evelyn was weak and Julius was a wimp for not marrying a woman who was more his equal. *Like me.*

Neely's gaze moved just past Julius and landed on Gerald, Julius' brother and best man. He smiled, waved, blew a kiss, and mouthed, "We're next." He still didn't understand she had no interest in him beyond a date every now and then. Their relationship wouldn't end up where Evelyn and Julius' did.

Neely decided, as Evelyn and Julius took their vows, that for everything she'd been through, she was owed some payback. Julius rejected her for Evelyn. Evelyn chose to marry Julius even though she knew Neely cared for him. Her mother didn't put a stop to the madness. Her father decided she wasn't worthy of love. Everyone would know her pain. The pain of not being wanted, of not being accepted. The pain of betrayal and the pain of a lost love.

Dear Reader,

Thank you so much for reading *Something Else to Want*. I hope you enjoyed it. My prayer is that Neely's story will encourage you to live your dreams and be the person God intended you to be in spite of the expectations of others. If I achieve that goal, I have done my job. I know there are millions of other books you can spend your time reading. I am honored that you chose to read one of mine.

Writing a book without someone to read it is pointless. That's why you, the reader, are so important. Your reviews, recommendations, and social media "shares" and "likes" are like fuel to an author.

If you enjoyed this book, please consider writing a review on the online retailer website of your choice. Also, visit me at my website, www.DarlissBatchelor.com. There you'll learn about my other books, read excerpts, see video and much more. You will also have the opportunity to sign up for updates which gives you access to exclusive content, early release information, discounts and freebies.

Until the next book,

Darliss Batchelor

P.S. You can also find me on the web:
Website: www.DarlissBatchelor.com
Amazon Author Page: www.amazon.com/author/DarlissBatchelor
Goodreads: www.Goodreads.com/DarlissBatchelor

Can't get enough of Neely?

Enjoy an excerpt from the novelette,

Demetri's Diary (*formerly Hell is a Skyscraper*)

from the book *Hell is a Skyscraper: A Trio of Novelettes*

# Chapter 1

"Evelyn, I'm going over to Neely's to fix something at her place."

"This late? Why can't you do it tomorrow?"

"She called me yesterday and I just didn't make it over there. It sounded important."

"All right then. Get on back as soon as possible."

Walking to his wife and giving her a peck on the lips, he responded, "I'll be right back." Leaving their half of the duplex, Julius stopped, remembering something else he needed to address with Evelyn. "I might as well pay the rent while I'm there. Do you have it?"

Evelyn slowly pushed herself out of her chair. She went to their bedroom to get her purse and retrieve the money for the rent.

Why her parents left this duplex to her sister, Neely, she didn't understand. For some reason, they thought Neely was a better choice to care for the family's home when they passed away.

When Evelyn questioned their wishes, her mother told her it was her father's decision, while her father claimed it was her mother's choice.

Evelyn's feelings were hurt when she found out Neely would take over the family home where they all grew up. It didn't matter now whose decision it was, Evelyn and her family needed a place to live and this was it. At least Neely allowed them to move in after their eviction from their previous rented home.

However, Neely could be so unreasonable about their rent being on time and the exact amount. If they were a penny short or a day late, she would lose her head and threaten to put her, Julius, and her children out on the street. Whether Neely would really follow through with her threat Evelyn wasn't sure, but she was certainly convincing if she was bluffing. With her husband barely working and her disability check being so small, she had to cut corners where necessary to make ends meet while satisfying Neely's demands.

Like tonight, Neely always had a chore or something for Julius to do. If it wasn't Julius, it was their son Demetri. Evelyn often wondered why Neely didn't get one of her many boyfriends to make repairs for her. Certainly, one of them was handy. Evelyn concluded Neely just liked having her brother-in-law and nephew jump whenever she called.

Evelyn suspected her sister was jealous of the fact that she was married and Neely had never been. Being the older sister and the more outgoing of the two, most would have thought Neely would be married first. However, Neely never had the privilege of experiencing even one proposal though she dated half the male population in their small town.

Evelyn hobbled back to the living room and gave the money to Julius so he could take it to Neely. She hoped he remembered to get a receipt so they would have proof of the cash payment. Evelyn never knew when Neely was going to try to get one over on them. A person couldn't put very much past Neely.

With Julius gone, Evelyn went in search of her nine-year-old son, Demetri. Vanessa, Demetri's thirteen-year-old sister, had long outgrown the bedtime ritual Evelyn was seeking her son for. She walked into her daughter's room thinking she might find him there, but Vanessa was its only inhabitant. She walked past the bathroom thinking she might find him in her bedroom. Suddenly, she heard his voice in the bathroom, stopping her in her tracks. She wondered to whom he was talking. Placing her ear close to the door, she realized he was talking to God. Feeling as though she shouldn't infringe on his privacy, she started to walk away. However, when she heard him crying, she returned to knock on the door.

"Demetri, are you in there?"

Demetri sniffled and responded, "Yes." It was obvious he tried to remove the tears from his voice, but his mother wasn't fooled. She'd already heard him crying.

"When you're done, come out to the living room. I have a special story for you tonight."

"I'll be there in a few minutes, Momma."

Evelyn had noticed her son's sadness on several occasions before now. She'd asked him if everything was okay and he'd assured her everything was fine. She didn't believe him because she knew him better than he knew himself. But with no input from him, it was difficult to help if she didn't know what the problem was. She'd been praying about this particular situation from the moment she first noticed the change in his demeanor.

Evelyn felt led to talk to her son even more about God's love in situations that may not be the best. She was going to talk to him about Joseph tonight because that was what she believed God was directing her to do. She didn't understand it all, but she knew well enough to be obedient to what she believed was God's direction regardless.

Eventually Demetri showed up for their nightly ritual, reading bible stories, praying, or whatever the two decided to do during "their time." His eyes were a bit puffy still and his nose a little red, but he did his best to hide his feelings. He crawled up next to his mother and snuggled up. She hugged him back and the two sat in silence for a brief period. There was silent communication between them. His mother confirmed her love for him and he let her know he believed her.

"Demetri, is there anything special you want to talk about tonight?"

Demetri looked as though he thought about saying something but quickly changed his mind and shook his head. Evelyn was disappointed because she knew something was going on and wanted desperately to help her son with whatever it was. She did take comfort in knowing he went to God with his concerns. Ultimately, it would take God to fix it regardless of who knew anyway, but it was natural for a mother to want to get involved as well.

"Do you remember when we talked about Joseph before?"

"Did he have that coat with all those colors?"

"That's him. God had a very special assignment for him. He spoke to Joseph through dreams."

"His dreams got him into trouble, didn't they?"

"Well, his brothers were angry because of a dream he had."

"Then they made him a slave."

"Yes, they did. He had many bad things happen to him after that. But, God still spoke to him through his dreams and visions. In the end, Joseph ended up right where God wanted him to be. You have a special assignment from God, too. We don't know exactly what it is yet, but I know it's there. Do you know what that assignment is called?"

"It's my calling."

"Yes, baby, it's your calling. I see you have been paying attention to me, haven't you?"

"Yes, Momma, I always listen to you. I'm not like Vanessa."

"I know, Demetri. I want you to remember that when things get hard and you go through difficult situations, it's part of the preparation for your calling. Don't be afraid. God is always with you. Momma and Daddy may not be there, but He will be. In the end, no matter what you go through, you'll get to the place where God wants you."

"What kind of difficult situations?"

"I don't know, but I think you're going through one now."

Demetri looked away from his mother once again at the mention of his problem. Again, he looked as though he debated telling his mother the nature of the issue.

"I am, Momma. But you taught me to talk to God about it and that's what I've been doing. Now I understand it might be because of my calling."

"That's right, baby. It's because of your calling.